ALWAYS CRASHING

ISSUE ONE

CHICAGO & URBANA, ILLINOIS • PITTSBURGH, PENNSYLVANIA

ISBN: 978-0-692-07002-4

Always Crashing is a magazine of fiction, poetry, and nameless things around and in-between. We publish one print issue per year and feature online content year-round. We are headquartered in Chicago and Urbana, Illinois, and Pittsburgh, Pennsylvania.

Editors: Jessica Berger & James Tadd Adcox

Managing Editor: Helenmary Sheridan

For submission guidelines, ordering information, and access to our electronic edition featuring new work every two weeks, please visit www.alwayscrashing.com

BOOM

/ Michael Martone

Serious mining of the natural gas reservoir, a reserve that would become known as the Trenton Field in east central Indiana, began in the late 1880s. Overnight, thousands of wells were drilled. The deposits of fossil fuel in the huge interconnected field spread over 5,000 square miles, nearly the size of the state of Connecticut, contained a trillion cubic feet of gas and a billion barrels of oil. To prove that the gas was flowing from the new well bores, the operators tapped the mainline, piping off a portion of the flow to set the surplus spectacularly ablaze. The flames towered over the plains and prairies, forests of fire. The flares could be seen as far north as Fort Wayne. And the light over the horizon above Indianapolis roiled and flickered, a manmade display of the aurora borealis. These constantly combusting gas flares came to be known as "Flambeau." The discovery led to an industrial boom for commerce, illumination, manufacturing, especially of glass products. Ball Brothers, Henry, Hoosier, Root, and Sneath—all these companies were attracted by the cheap and seemingly inexhaustible fuel. Art Smith, The Bird Boy of Fort Wayne, began his flying career just as the great gas field of Indiana was reaching its peak. Aloft, even in daylight, he could see over the horizon, south to the far reaches of Delaware, Jay, Blackford, and Grant Counties and the copses of yellow orange flames flaring in the distance, the light seemingly floating, like oil on the shimmering melting azure of liquefied air. At night, the Flambeau burning created a deep blue mirage, a blanket that wavered like waves on a black sand shore. In 1912, the Chamber of Commerce of Gas City hired Smith to celebrate The Boom by writing BOOM over the booming city ringed with flaming groves and arbors of Flambeau whose jets of combusting gases leapt up toward Smith's vapory writerly combustion, fingers pointing, twitching flickering hands grasping the slowly expanding, ever thinning rings of the mute BOOM.

BOO

/ Michael Martone

Only a few years later, Art Smith, The Bird Boy of Fort Wayne, returned to the famous Trenton Gas Field on a more sober mission of sky calligraphy. The pressure across the field was falling. The decline in pressure meant that the gas to heat the houses and power the furnaces of Indiana would soon be too low to continue flowing. At the turn of the century the pressure at the wellheads was near 200 psi. By the time of Smith's initial visit, the flow had fallen to 150 psi and continued to fall. It was suspected, even then, that the open displays of flame were a major contribution to the rapid depletion of what was thought to be a vast and bottomless resource. Now, a century later, we understand that as much as 90% of the field's natural gas was wasted in Flambeau displays. And much of the proved oil reserve, without the pressurized gas to aid in its extraction, remains below the Hoosier bog unlifted and unliftable. In 1916, Smith was invited back to Indiana (from his triumphant turn at the Panama–Pacific Exposition in San Francisco where he had lit up the night with skywriting, produced by means of phosphoric flares) to commemorate the extinguishing of the final Flambeau. The fire forests of standing pipe, burning continuously for a quarter of a century, now saw their arboreal canopy of flame dwindling, going out, extinguished. The Chamber of Commerce at Gas City did not want to wait for what now seemed to be inevitable, but instead sought to ceremonially cap what was believed to be the last Flambeau. This they did as Art Smith arched over the funereal crowd below. He considered writing "DOUSE" or "DONE" or "ENOUGH' or "SNUFF" or "OVER." He wanted to find a word that would suggest the blowing out of candles on a birthday cake, onomatopoeia of exhaustion, exhalation, breath, a whooshing whispered wish. But he settled on a return to the optimistic BOOM of a few years before, transmuted to this startled interjection of the unexpected, the uncontrolled. The sun was setting as he took to the air. The Indiana

State Seal depicts a sun near a mountainous horizon, a man with an ax felling a tree that a bison leaps over in flight. There was never much thought about the kind of sun that's pictured, setting or rising. But now? And the mountains in the distance, they never made sense, he thought, as he closed the last radii of his second zero and the faint sun sank through it toward the flat, hairline fracture that would be there in the diminished distance, Illinois.

ALL YOUR MOST PRIVATE PLACES

/ Meghan Lamb

They drive together through the night. They roll the windows down. The air surrounds them as they're driving through the desert. It's everything. It's what they hear. The wind made by their movement. Wheels on asphalt. Pinkish river-pool of neon lights receding.

It's the city. He turns up the headlights, turning down the radio. The static crackles, gravel, road fades into dust. The road becomes each line of white revealed by the headlights. Great black jaws of mountain swallowing the swimming pools of pink.

She thinks, the city feels like a volcano. It is not the first time she has had this thought. She feels foggy. Sweating. It's the desert heat. Volcano. Neon lava. Or whatever. But, she thinks, there's more to it than that.

You want the radio? he says.

Not really. She's not listening.

He says, me neither. He's not listening. He turns it off.

The city feels dormant in the day. The neon lights are not yet lit, but they're still felt. She feels this pulse. This throb of buildings pumping false metallic air. The cooling which she understands creates a greater heat.

As they drive from the city, she thinks, it is strange just how easy it seems when you're driving away. In the daytime, when lights are just rhythms, she feels like the city is all that there is.

*

In the darkness, the desert is always erupting. It's something that everyone knows. It's a looming, their knowledge, these dark crags, this bright neon magma, this charge to the air. The night sky smells like sagebrush, sand, which is to say, this powder, ammunition, dust. The smell of heat. The cactus flowers bloom.

Meanwhile, a line of cars pulls into Station UA1. The station workers scan their cards. The gate goes up and down. A sign above the gate says: An Environmental Research Park. The sign below that says: Buckle up. It's the law.

The workers wait there in their line of cars, sipping their coffee from plastic or tin tubes, styrofoam or paper cups. They check the time. They clear their throats. They yawn. They stretch in place. They sift around in pockets for their ID cards.

They look out of their windows and they wait. Long black lines of lamps cast cold white lines of light.

Their own white jackets sit beside them, folded into rectangles. They wait. They have so many sets of clean white jackets just like these. They sip their coffee, think of stains. These clean white surfaces. Such a responsibility. They think, it is only a matter of time.

They sit there, sipping. The beginning of another day. They think of darkness turning into white, try not to think of stains. They think of home. They think of pulling their clean jackets from the wash. The soft clean smell. They're like spare sheets for some strange guest who never seems to leave.

*

They feel this unnameable dread when he pulls their car into the driveway. It's the sound of splintered blacktop, hissing. Then, the way it stops. The respiration of exhaust, for just a moment. Then, the way it stops completely. Then, the feeling they are home. They have arrived.

They take off their clothes and they mill toward the bedroom. She waits for him by the window, palms flattened against the ledge. She hears him click the light on, so she squints. He comes up from behind. He puts his hands upon her hands and presses her into the glass.

The blonde-lit linen drapes move as their bodies move. The edges stick. She grips the ledge. She looks. She peers outward into the night.

She sees the feathered silhouette of their acacia tree. Then, she sees fog. She squints. Then, fog. Then, branches. Fog. Then, branches. Fog. Then, branches.

She closes her eyes. Her nipples rub against the linen. Sweat gleams on her stomach. She feels like she's floating, falling, into nothingness.

Her hands slip from the ledge. He grabs her hands. He grabs her wrists. He grabs her arms. He grabs her legs. He gasps. He comes.

They lie together on the bed. She's turned toward the window. He clicks off the light. He's turned toward her back.

Good night, my dear, he tells her back.

Good night, she tells the window.

I love you, he tells her back.

I love you too, she tells the window.

*

The tourists turn to face the viewing platform. Its window is the front wall of UA1's so-called bunker. The tour director, Lee, directs them to the glass, assures them it is bullet-proof. The bunker's built to standard. Whatever that means.

Lee distributes small plastic binoculars to the tourists. He directs them to the model subdivision. Rows of square lawns, picket fences, and split-level houses. Built to standard. Desert stretches out on every side.

It's called Survivor City, he explains. The tourists murmur-nod with grave expressions, like this means something to them. The window's amber tinted, so the light looks gold. It frames the subdivision with a soft, uncanny glow.

It has a retro look, a tourist says.

Another tourist says, it's like a 50s photograph. Looks like my mother's neighborhood.

A man in a Hawaiian shirt is really getting into it. He says, I feel like I've stepped back into another time.

Lee shakes his head. He says, it's not another time. It's meant to look like anywhere in any time. Timeless, in other words.

The man says, Lee. He looks at him like, I don't know you. He says, Lee, I think I know what I am feeling when I feel it.

Lee does not respond. He details the history of the museum, the legacy of the test site, the ways that it has changed throughout the years. He leads them through a hallway filled with stainless steel beams, then ducks them down into a tunnel filled with pipes. Some pipes emit a slight sulfuric smell. Please watch your heads, he says, directing them to shelves of safety goggles and hard hats.

The tunnel begins to get dark, but there are headlamps on the hats. The on switch is on the left side, Lee tells the tourists. Click, click, click, click. The clicking echoes like the dripping of a cavern wall. The dim-lit tunnel flickers like a line of lightning bugs.

Eventually, the tunnel opens out into a larger viewing platform filled with many periscopes. Lee tells the tourists they're invited to look through the periscopes, to get a clearer picture of Survivor City.

Are those people in the houses? someone inevitably asks.

Lee shakes his head. Test figures. In a minute, I will demonstrate.

The periscopes allow the tourists to peer into the model houses. Through the windows, they can see the ways the figures were arranged.

One model home reveals a set of figures in the living room. Two child-size figures sit together on the love seat. A man-size figure lounges in an armchair by the floor lamp with a glass beside him and a magazine spread on his lap.

A woman figure in a dress stands by the window. She is close enough for tourists to gaze at the details of her face. She wears her hair styled in a simple mid-length bob. She has long, black-lined lashes, blue eyes, and a pale sort of almost-smile.

Survivor City is outlined with huge ominous craters. From this angle, now, within the periscopes, their full scale is revealed. Most craters are the size of many houses. If they panned in closer, in the corner, they would see a tortoise peeking from its shell.

Do they use real nukes? Hawaiian shirt man asks.

Lee says, of course not, no. They don't use nuclear explosives. They have not conducted real tests in decades. Things are different, now, he says. This is a research park. They're simply recreating an experience.

So, they're not real nukes? the shirt man says.

Lee says, they're not. They're meant to look and act as much like real nukes as possible.

Lee does not like to hear himself answer this question. In all honesty, he doesn't know what happens at this site. He's never seen the real testing site, the part that's confidential. When he asked his boss about it, he was vague and cagey.

That's not your job, he said. That part is science. Visitors don't come for science. That is not what they are looking for.

What are they looking for? Lee glanced down at his boss's gun belt, then quickly looked back up into his gleaming metal badge.

They want reassurance. They're just making sense of things, he said. This gives a good face. Humanizes the whole operation.

Lee's boss moved closer, then. He noticed he smelled slightly musky and his breath had just a bit of an acidic tinge. He patted his hand on Lee's shoulder. You do good, he said. You do important work. It is important to preserve our own humanity.

*

He looks across the table at his wife as they eat breakfast, which is flaxseed waffles served with slices of banana. She's arranged the waffles on their avocado green Fiestaware, banana slices laid like petals on the plate.

She is wearing her work clothes, a powder blue shirt dress with buttons buttoned to the neck. It is classy, he thinks. There's a small gap between the two buttons above and right below her breasts. He can see a slight trace of her bra. He thinks that this is sexy. She looks at him while she is sipping her coffee. She raises one eyebrow. He raises one eyebrow. He thinks, she is classy, but sexy.

He has this fantasy. He thinks about it often, but he hasn't brought it up yet. He is waiting for the right time.

He looks down and scrapes his waffles. She gets up and takes the plates. Her heels click. The water hisses. Plates clink. Now is not the right time.

In his fantasy, they find a local call girl from an ad. They call the number. They tell her what they are thinking. She tells them she is excited. She senses they are attractive. Classy/sexy. Something he thinks that call girls are not used to.

This is all part of the fantasy, this need to give her something. They provide the call girl with something exceptional. They're not just there to give her money. She enjoys herself. She feels relaxed. They talk together and they listen to some music.

He pours champagne. When the call girl finishes her glass, she gets a look. She leans in toward his wife and starts unbuttoning her dress. Her eyes are on that gap between the buttons. The call girl is wearing something slutty, something that his wife would never wear.

He asks, is it okay if I take pictures? She says, yes, of course. Please feel free. As many as you need. He snaps a picture of the girl unbuttoning his wife's dress, panning in on her expression, capturing her smile. He takes a picture of them kissing as their bodies fold together, capturing her smile as it melts in someone else's mouth.

*

Lee says, now, count down from 10. The tourists glance up, back, and forth. They clutch their wrists. Hawaiian shirt man's dripping sweat. 10, 9, 8, 7, 6, 5, 4, 3, 2, 1. Silence. Light. Explosion.

They see the flash before they hear the sound, which is so deep, it barely registers as what they know it is. There is a second flash. The shutters and the roof tops seem to splash in one direction, riding on the arc of an invisible wave.

The windows shatter. Paint begins to blister, bubble, singe. The edges of the roof are licked with tiny temporary flames. The flames burn quickly. All the houses stand just as they stood. It is a testament to standards, Lee says, how well they were built.

The tourists look out through the periscopes. They see the figures in the houses were not harmed. Although, the fringes of the woman's bangs are black. Her lashes charred and feathered. Bits of glass gleam on her shoulders like scattered necklace.

One of the children now leans to the side, like she is pulling back. The man leans forward, like he's doubled over in some kind of shock. What does this mean, they think, this delicate destruction? Tourists file toward the exit. They do not know what this means.

They fiddle with their pamphlets. Thanks and come again. You're welcome. They came here to learn something. They don't remember. They leave, feeling they've learned nothing. They pull out onto the desert highway, turn the AC up, turn on the radio. Hawaiian shirt man says, it was a museum. That is how they did things in the past. His wife nods and the desert stretches all around them. He says, honestly, we've come a long way. The sun glares. He adjusts the mirrors. He smiles at his wife. They are relieved, but disappointed.

*

There is a moment in her drive to work that always catches her. It is the moment where the highway meets the turnoff to the desert. It's the turnoff that they take on their long night drives. She has never driven on this desert route during the day.

She thinks of driving through the desert to wherever. Gnarled scraps of brush and cactus trees, cracked spiderwebs of dirt becoming graceful slopes of dunes, becoming sky, becoming nothing, nothing but potentialities that she cannot envision.

*

Instead, she pulls off at the donut shop. She buys two mixed dozens and a box of coffee. The pink cardboard sits beside her. Its smells sweet and sticky. Sticking her to what she needs to do and where she needs to go.

What does she need to do? Where does she need to go? She barely knows, these days, but it involves getting their coffee and their donuts. She deposits them onto a table in the break room with a note. Please take one, says the note. She draws a smiley face. The smiley face's eyes are spread too far apart. She feels that this makes it look a little crazed and desperate.

At her desk, she edits photos of rich people at events. She blurs and touches up and does what's needed to make them look good. Most of the women wear these shelf-like strapless dresses. They look stupid. They're intended to be flattering, but everyone looks fat. Nobody understands themselves, she thinks, fixing the images. She thinks, it's posturing. The things they do to make themselves look classy.

*

He looks out onto an overwatered golf course. He can hear the sprinklers run throughout the day. He forgets them for short intervals while sending e-mails, processing new data, or setting reminders on his calendar. After awhile, he pauses and looks out of the window. He hears three spritzes of water, a short revolution, six thin sprits of water, then a revolution, then one longer, louder stream of water, then a revolution, back to the beginning.

Sometimes, he looks beyond the golf course to the mountains, which stand, looking back at him, above the false green slopes. In the morning, they're violet flickers emerging from lavender clouds. By midday, they've unfolded a gold-green expanse that recedes into shadows of blue. By the end of the work day, the sky has accumulated a thick yellowish haze. He powers down, flicks off the lights, and stands to close the blinds. He thinks, I have changed through the years in all these ways I can't articulate. The mountains always still themselves, a looming gray suggestion.

*

As a child, he spent a lot of time inside his best friend's partially finished basement, on the unfinished side, exploring stacks of Playboys. They both sat on these rickety metal-frame lawn chairs. They drank Diet Rite because that's what they had. The crushed cans piled up. The basement smelled like dirty socks.

He was filled with a sense of discovery then. It had little to do with the images. The women were okay, but they mostly looked the same. The pictures blended with the sound of turning pages. The sense of discovery came from the things that they found themselves saying.

I like that one, his friend pointed out. I like when they have puffy nipples.

Puffy? he said.

Yeah, his friend said. When they look like that.

He asked, what do you call them, then, when they're not puffy?

I don't know. He shrugged. He crushed his can. Just regular, I guess.

I like that one, he said. The red lace panties.

His friend nodded his approval. Yeah. All girls look good in red.

I guess they do, he thought. He spent a silent moment thinking, why? I like how bright it is, he said. It just stands out.

This way, they both established their taxonomy of parts, their lexicon for subtle preferences in color, size, and shape.

*

While driving home, he thinks of Diet Rite and red lace panties. He thinks about his wife, how she is beautiful. He's lucky. He wants to share that sense of mutual discovery. He wants to see what she sees, create a shared language.

*

As a child, his wife was frightened of discovery. She was a quiet girl. That's what her mother said. She preferred empty spaces; after all, she lived within the desert. She should've been able to be happy where she was.

It doesn't work like that, her mother said. She told her, in a perfect world. She sighed, of course, because the world wasn't perfect. She felt her pocket with the lipstick and the box of cigarettes. She pulled two sticks of spearmint gum out of the other pocket. In a perfect world, we'd all get what we want, she said, but we don't really even know exactly what we want, most of the time.

Her mother took her swimming. She'd swim while her mother lounged beside the pool. She crawled out of the pool whenever she felt hungry. Pool water seems to designed to make you hungry, she complained. Her mother told her to be patient. She was happy lying in the sun. She tried to lie there with her mother, but her body felt exposed, so she turned over on her stomach, spread a towel on her back. She felt her stomach pinched between the plastic chair slats. She looked through the space between the slats and watched a spider drowning in a puddle.

She went to slumber parties where they looked at magazines. The magazines asked questions about what they wanted, who they could become. Could you be a model? the magazine articles asked. Could I be a model? the girls at the parties would ask themselves. They didn't know. It seemed like a good question.

They stashed the pizza boxes in a greasy corner by the trash. They dug around the junk drawer with this stupid urgency. They found the measuring tape tucked inside an old tin can of cookies from the days when cookies always came in old tin cans.

The girls lined up—they actually lined up—and a girl would measure ankles, wrists, waists, leg length, shoulder width, hips, height, and neck circumference, comparing their measurements to lists of model ranges in the magazines, the standard units used within the industry.

As it turned out, none of them could have been models. Some girls came close in some ways but fell short in others. They were tall enough, but their hips were too wide. Their waists were small enough, but they had scrawny calves or weird thick ankles. Their shoulder width, hips, waist, were all in perfect ratio, but for some reason, one leg was a little longer than the other.

*

While driving home, she thinks of how she hates her insecurities. They're childish, of course. They haven't changed since childhood. She contemplates this concept, childhood. When did it end? She looks out at the endless desert, thinking that it never did.

*

Meanwhile, something horrible is happening at the test site. Not UA1. The real site, the site that uses nukes. They're building new machines that detonate from deep within the earth. Enormous black cables extend in all directions.

These new machines do not leave cratered surfaces. These new machines do not create plume clouds of dust. The explosions of these new machines appear to be invisible. Their damage—unseen and unreachable—is hard to estimate.

Somewhere inside the night, the figures of a man and woman wait inside a model bedroom in a model home. The man lies, turned toward the woman's back, his arms around her waist. The woman lies, turned toward the window, palms clasped underneath her head.

Good night, my dear, the male figure tells the woman's back.

Good night, the woman figure tells the model window.

Good night, the long black cable tunnels whisper through inaudible uncanny tremors they can somehow hear.

I love you, he tells her back.

I love you too, she tells the window.

I love you too, the long black cable tunnels tell them. As the neon glow begins to rise, the summer insects drone. The long black cable tunnels swarm with the unseen.

*

As a child, Lee only liked to masturbate in bed. Whenever he came, he would wipe the leavings underneath his bed frame. He was not sure why he did this, but he didn't think to stop, once he began. It was a ritual that had to be fulfilled.

One day when Lee came home from school, he saw his mother crouched beside the bed, wearing an apron and a pair of yellow gloves. Her gloved hands reached beneath the mattress, scrubbing down the frame. White soapy streams of something dripped into a metal bucket.

He said nothing. She said nothing, even when she finished cleaning, but she placed a box of tissues on his bedside table.

That night, as he drifted off to sleep, he listened to the sounds of traffic curving through a nearby stretch of highway. He felt empty, in his bed. His bed felt empty and he thought about the bucket, being filled with little bits of him. He closed his eyes. He didn't understand why he felt lonely. He had not imagined how much he could miss his own accumulation.

*

Lee lies in bed now thinking of the real test site thinking how his thoughts are now this fear that slowly seeps and builds into this feeling that explodes when he's alone inside the darkness and attaches itself permanently to the underside of his bed.

*

Tonight, they are having sex in bed. They tangle their sand-colored sheets into the shapes of miniature dunes. He twists her legs around him, bends her knees, lifts them and lowers them. She lifts herself and lowers herself down. She sweeps her hands along the mini sand dunes. Sweat sticks to his forehead. She licks it. He kisses her. She accidentally butts his chin.

They lie in bed. He's looking at her back. She's looking at the window and they almost fade into the old routine. But there's this feeling in his stomach, this electric buzz that shocks him intermittently. It's giving him a sense of clarity. Now is the time. He says, I have this fantasy. His wife turns over in bed and she faces him. She gives her full attention.

*

15 minutes later, she is standing in front of the vanity. She's rubbing cotton balls of creamy liquid on her body. He says, look, we do not have to do this. We don't have to do this right away. She's rubbing really, really frantically.

He says, are you okay?

She looks back in the mirror. I'm fine.

He rolls his eyes.

She says, I'm fine.

He repeats, we don't have to do this.

She throws down her cotton ball. It's hard to throw dramatically. She covers her face with both her hands and cries.

She says, I'm sorry. No, I want to. No, I do, I promise.

After a minute, she says, is it me, or is it really hot?

*

It is really hot that night. A couple miles away, a woman passes out beside a dumpster in an alley. The last thing she sees before she dies is dumpster lid. The last thing she smells is a heat wave of dumpster rising up into her face.

Nobody sees her. No one knows her when they find her. No one calls to claim connection to her body or her life.

*

15 minutes later, they are looking at the laptop in bed, clicking through the profiles on various escort sites. The women are categorized into Blonde, Brunette, Asian, Redhead, and Ebony. Some escort profiles are labeled as product descriptions. The product descriptions make promises. One product promises, if you look into her eyes, you'll fall prey to her sweet spell of seduction. One prod-

uct promises she has an unmatched appetite for sexual experiences beyond your wildest dreams. One product promises she'll make those dreams reality, says she will gladly listen to whatever you desire. She says she will go to all your most private places. She says she will fulfill you, physically and mentally.

*

The next morning, she absently chews on a donut while editing photos. She is editing a picture of an average-looking woman. She licks powdered sugar from her lips and analyzes which features construct this average-looking woman's averageness.

The woman's wearing average-looking clothes (a shelf-like strapless dress). The woman wears an average-looking hairstyle (artificially straightened bob). The woman has an average-seeming body, not too thin or heavy, not too short or tall (she could be wearing heels beneath her dress). The woman has some pretty features (full lips, high cheekbones), some noticeable flaws (a weak jawline, an oddly upturned nose). She looks down at her empty napkin, wondering when and how she came to be the arbiter of who and what is average.

*

He goes to the office bathroom to look in the mirror. It is a private bathroom. You must have a key to get inside. This privacy affords him time. He doesn't need much time. He studies his eyes, nose, and mouth, evaluates his jawline, lifts his shirt and turns, moves close, steps back, and makes a couple different faces. He nods. Just as he expected, he's an average-looking man.

*

When they come home from work, they view more escort profiles. They notice one they both like called Leelani. In her pictures, she is wearing red lace panties. She is posing in the gold-lit glow of what appears to be a luxury hotel.

I like that one, he tells her. The red lace panties.

His wife nods. All girls look good in red. She presses her red lips together.

Puffy nipples, too, he says.

His wife nods.

Perky breasts.

She nods. The profile mentions she's a spinner. Do you know what that means?

He says, a spinner is a petite girl. She's really light. Easy to spin on your cock.

She looks blank. He doesn't know what her expression means.

He explains, you can switch from front to back without needing to pull out.

She says, oh. She now knows what a spinner is.

There is a level to this research she enjoys. In many ways, it is an interesting inversion of her job. She smiles for him but he doesn't see her smile. The laptop glow reflects into his glasses, turning them to silent screens.

*

Leelani lives in a month-to-month rental on the other side of the city. Leelani is not this woman's real name. She is not the woman in the pictures, either. She's a woman with a couple features comparable to the pictures.

She is one of three women the agency currently uses to portray the part of Leelani. These women come and go. Leelanis come and go.

In this moment, she is out of character, crouched on her bed. She's watching *Die Hard* on a grainy television screen. She's in her underwear, which is a pair of blue-striped cotton Hanes and a white t-shirt with a city name she has no real connection to.

She is painting her nails a shade of dark shimmery slate blue. The name of the polish she uses is Tough As Nails. She thinks about an article she read once—she can't recall where—about nails, how nails, hair, and skin are all made of the same thing.

She blows on her nails and they bristle. Her hair stands on its edges. Yippie ki yay, motherfuckers, she whispers into the static.

She waves her hands to dry them. Something's creeping in her stomach. Hunger. Loneliness. Who knows. She swallows hard.

She waves her fingers back and forth like little wings. Her nails look good.

She smiles as the helicopter explodes.

*

It's called Survivor City, Lee tells a new crowd. The new group nods. A new Hawaiian shirt man queries him about the nukes. They're meant to look and act as real as possible, he now explains. They now look through the periscopes into another room.

It is a bedroom with a man and woman lying in their bed. The woman's turned toward the window, looking out at them. Her gaze now meets the tourists' gaze. Some tourists back off from the periscopes. The scene looks too familiar, feels too voyeuristic.

*

Her fantasy is simple. She tells herself it's simple. She tells herself she has no expectations.

She has expectations. Everybody does.

Okay, she knows.

Okay, she tells herself, maybe it's not that simple.

In her fantasy, the call girl's pretty in a different way from her.

But not too pretty.

Not too different.

It's hard to explain.

She's pretty in a way that they can both relate to, but they both relate to her in separate, different, and unspoken ways.

She looks at her like, we're both women, and that means something.

She doesn't know what it means, what it should mean, what she wants for it to mean.

She knows she doesn't want the call girl to be prettier than her. She doesn't want to look at her and feel inferior.

She wants to feel attraction to her and connection with her and she wants her husband to experience attraction and connection.

But she wants a firm before, during, and after, a firm cut off, for her husband to feel, afterward, they both have everything they need.

*

He calls the agency from his car on his lunch break. A woman answers, asks what she can do for him. She has just a hint of an accent he can't trace. He tells her that he wants to book Leelani.

Is she available tonight? he asks.

She says, please hold on, darling. Just a moment. He can hear another phone ring in the background. He hears her shuffle, pick up, and the muffled vagueness of her voice. A moment later, shuffle, pick up, she returns.

Yes, dear, she says. Thank you for waiting. Yes, she can see you tonight.

What are her rates? he asks. The website doesn't specify.

250 gets her there and comfortable, she says. Whatever happens after that is up to you, of course.

The pictures on the site, he clears his throat. The pictures on the site—are those an accurate reflection of what she looks like?

An accurate reflection, she repeats. Her voice sounds like it's smiling. Absolutely, yes, of course. I should be honest though. We use a model photograph, she says. We use a model to protect the girls. Their privacy, she says.

He says, I understand.

Our girls are beautiful, she says. Leelani is a classy lady, much more beautiful and lovely than a picture.

I have another question, he says. Does she work with couples?

Let me check, she says. He hears more shuffling and another muffled voice. The phone receiver rustles against something when her voice returns. She tells him, yes. She sounds excited to deliver the good news.

I am booking a date with my wife, he explains.

Ah, she says. That will be good. The pitch of her voice rises. And your wife, she says, does she like pretty ladies?

He thinks for a moment. Yes, she does, he says.

Leelani is a pretty lady, she says. Very pretty. He provides his address and he books the date. That's good. You and your wife are going to have a good time, she says. Can I do anything else for you? Baby? she adds, a bit too late.

He pauses. Yes, he realizes. Can she wear something specific?

Of course, baby, she says. This time it sounds much more natural.

Please ask her to wear red lace panties, he says.

Absolutely. Red lace panties, she repeats. I will have her wear them for you.

He hangs up and unwraps his takeout salad in the car. He peels off the plastic lid, peels off a second sealed layer. He tears the dotted line along the dressing packet, pours it on, and stirs it through the salad with a plastic spork. The salad is okay. He squeezes out more dressing. He chews slowly, moving bits of every bite he takes inside his mouth. The texture feels weirdly uniform. Well, what does he expect? He thinks, that is the key: adjust your expectations.

*

She gets home early and she walks into the bedroom. She pulls three dresses from the closet, spreads them out across the bed. She then arranges them with corresponding objects, panties, stockings, garter belts, and different pairs of matching heeled shoes.

She stands against the closet door to contemplate the dresses. She thinks they look like little shadow people. They're waiting for a human form to fill them, to make sense of them. They're waiting for a human form to be fulfilled.

She looks and can't remember when or where she wore these dresses. She looks and feels like she's never seen them. She feels like they all belong to separate shadow bodies. Faceless, featureless. Unknown, unknowable.

*

Lee says, now, count down from 10. The tourists glance up, back, and forth. The figures in the bedroom wait there, helplessly. 10, 9, 8, 7, 6, 5, 4, 3, 2, 1. Silence. Light. Explosion.

Something goes wrong. Something has gone wrong and the house goes up. The flicker flames burst into streamers into banners into clouds of billow bulbs of terrible terrific toxic fire. The whole house is engulfed. The tourists gasp. Is this a test? Is this supposed to happen?

Lee's eyes widen. He grabs for a phone against the wall. He speaks a numbered code. A muffled voice says, yes. It will be dealt with.

Lee instructs the tourists to please remain calm. Yes, yes, of course, this is a test. There is no need to worry. They are miles from the fire. Remember, when you look into the periscope, the things you see appear much closer to you than they really are.

The fire burns out on its own within a couple minutes. Where the house stood, there is now a crater pit of blackened smoke and dust. The crater is the only evidence that anything existed. In this space, the only evidence is absence.

The figures in the bedroom were just models, Lee reminds them. The house was just a model. Nothing in the house was real. The objects were not used. The rooms within its walls were untouched, once they were arranged. In short, he says, nothing about the house was human.

Inside the crater, tiny shapes are drifting, shapes and movements that the tourists' periscopes all fail to reveal. The shapes are skeletons of desert creatures, lizards, mice, and squirrels that made nests, made their own families within the model home.

*

She runs a bath. She stands behind the sink and stares into the mirror. She watches her reflection turn to vapors. Now, her face is just this foggy, vaguely colored pixelation. She thinks, somewhere, on some level, this is what I always am.

She gets into the hot bath and she tries to feel sexy. She is hoping that the haze of heat will turn her on. She lathers soap between her fingers, thinks of pinup photos of rich naked ladies with their nearly naked soapy-bubbled servants.

She drifts down deeper in the bath. The steamy water swirls. She breathes in, thinking of the preparations to be made. She thinks about how sex is getting clean, then getting dirty, getting clean, then getting dirty, on and on for your whole fucking life.

*

Meanwhile, Leelani prepares for their date. She too stands by the closet, pulling dresses and assessing them. Her choice is simple, though, as she has fewer options. All her clothes are either sexy clothes (for work) or lounging clothes (for private life.)

Leelani's private life does not resemble her profile. She mostly lives in bed, but that is incidental. She lives with a fan positioned toward the corner of the mattress where she crouches, watching television while she paints her nails.

*

She's putting on her lipstick by the mirror when he comes home. Bright red, of course. She dabs, purses her lips, and smiles at him.

She says, how was your day? It is a day like any other and it makes no difference what they're doing in a couple minutes.

He says, okay, and puts a bag of groceries on the counter. In the bag of groceries, there's a bottle of champagne. They do not drink.

She asks, so, what's the bottle for? She doesn't ask him, who.

He shrugs. I don't know. It's just classy, right, to have champagne?

She's putting on mascara, so she's making a strange face. She keeps her eyes wide open as she brushes them behind the mirror. She thinks, we all do stupid things to seem attractive. She says, classy, yes. You're right. It's good to have something to offer.

I made a mix, he says, to play while we, you know.

She nods.

He says, I'm going to play the first few tracks, make sure it sounds okay.

He plays the first track. It's a sexy R&B song filled with bass and female backup vocalists whose voices sound too shimmery.

He moves beside her in the mirror. He smiles and combs his hair. He unbuttons his shirt, sprays on cologne. He says, and, well?

She says, I don't know.

He says, what.

She says, eh.

He says, what.

She says, it's just. I don't know.

He says, what.

She says, it's just kind of intense. It sounds like you're trying to say something.

He buttons up his shirt. She screws the cap on her mascara.

He looks at her in the mirror. His look says, Jesus Christ. Give me a break.

We won't play music then, he says. No problem. Done.

Okay, she says.

It doesn't matter anyway, he says.

Okay, she says.

I'm going to brush my teeth, he says. My mouth tastes like a dumpster.

*

He brushes his teeth three times. His mouth just tastes so weird. He puts on more cologne. Why does he smell like shit tonight?

He clears his throat. He says, hey, look. His wife sits by him on the toilet. He says, I called the agency. The profile photo is a model.

She says, what does that mean?

He says, I'm not exactly sure. I just know she might look a little different from her photo.

She thinks of her job, the pictures that she edits. She says, oh.

He says, I know.

She shrugs. She says, I guess we'll see.

He nods in agreement. Yeah. I guess we'll see.

They hover there together, breathing in the scent of his cologne.

*

The agency calls. He picks up.

She says, Leelani's driving over. She'll be there in five minutes.

He tells her, thank you.

He puts the champagne on the table. He straightens the sheets. He says, dear, when the doorbell rings, please answer it for me, okay?

She tells him, sure.

He clears his throat. He swirls his spit around his mouth. His mouth tastes awful. He goes back into the bathroom and brushes his teeth.

*

Lee drives home through the desert. The gray sky turns lavender, then violet black. In the distance, he hears thunder as the sky becomes the sand, the road, the hills, the trees. The sky turns everything to shadows except for the white dashed line that separates the road.

The rain begins to pour. The white line, what he needs to follow, dashed against the road, a dotted line, a slit across the desert's throat. He thinks of long black cable tunnels, veins of toxic blood. He feels the underworld pulsing, pouring out into the open air.

Lee bites his lip. He wants to close his eyes as he pulls up into the mountains' mouth, the bright pink maw that is the city where he lives. The flashing signs, the buildings streaked with horizontal light incisions, liquid neon drizzles, gushing neon fountains. The palm trees are black silhouettes against the light, fronds blowing in the wind like charred hair, skirts, and flailing arms of captive women.

The lightning mingles with the neon. An electric sky. The city turns into a brilliant, burning, blazing bulb. The lightning plumes, conducting who knows what within the clouds. A lightning sky. The roots of some inverted flaming bush.

He parks his car. He locks the door. He holds his keys. Ignores his neighbor, slumped as usual against the slanted staircase. He unlocks the door. He locks the door. Turns on the light. Ignores the humming strip. Takes off his clothes. Turns off the light. Gets into bed.

For just one sacred moment, all is dark and all is silent. His room is his world, his own deep bluish sanctuary.

But then, the light seeps in. The rainbow light, reflected in the raindrops on the window. Sounds of rain against the glass. The sound of sirens. They remind him that the world goes on and on without him and he lives alone, alone, alone, alone.

*

The doorbell rings. She gets up. She looks through the peephole. There's a short thin woman standing by herself on her front door step. Her hand's clasped around her arm. Her tall shoes teetering. She looks up, back, and forth. She shifts her purse. She shifts her feet. Her hair is wet.

Leelani? she asks.

Yes, she says. They exchange nods.

Come in, she says. She opens up the door. The woman comes

inside the house.

She looks at Leelani. She looks nothing like her picture. She seems shorter and less evenly proportioned. She has dark rings underneath her eyes she's tried to hide with makeup. She has dozens of ambiguous tattoos.

She isn't unattractive. She is not someone who would stand out as unattractive in a picture she was editing at work. But she is also not someone who would stand out, especially. But here she is, standing in front of her inside her home, right now.

She hears her husband spit behind the bathroom door. She says, hello.

Leelani nods. Hello. How are you doing, tonight?

She says, I'm fine, thanks. She looks down. Please sit down, she suggests.

Leelani sits down in the middle of the sofa.

She says, would you like some champagne?

No thanks, says Leelani. I don't drink when seeing clients.

She thinks, oh. I am a client. Oh, of course, she says.

She hears the water run, then stop. The bathroom door opens.

Hello, her husband says.

Leelani says, hello.

Her husband sits down in the arm chair. He looks at his wife like, you're still standing. Go sit down. She sits next to Leelani. Looks like you caught the rain, her husband says.

Leelani nods. Storms are so sudden here, she says. They come so strong and then they vanish, just as quickly as they came.

You're not from here? her husband asks.

She smiles. No, I haven't been here long.

He asks, where are you from?

She shrugs. Around. All over.

Leelani glances back and forth at each of them.

She says, so, I'm assuming you guys haven't done this before?

It's our first time, he nods. And, what about you? Is this your first time, he adds, visiting a couple?

Leelani smiles like she thinks he's trying to deflect. It's not, she says. I've been with other couples before you.

She's trying not to notice that Leelani's hair smells overwhelmingly of hairspray, cheap perfume, and cigarettes.

Leelani says, so, I don't know how much the agency explained. The way this works is, you give me $250, and that gets me here. Now that I'm here, we'll talk about what you've been thinking, and I'll give you prices for the other services you'd like.

He looks at Leelani. Leelani looks at him. He thinks, her face looks blank. He feels off. He wanted her to like him. He feels disappointed. His wife thinks she looks expectant, but she's trying to conceal this behind a blankly feigned expression.

He says, just a moment. I'll go get the money from the bedroom.

She says, take your time, please. I am in no hurry.

*

She looks nothing like the photos, he says.

I am sorry, sir, a woman says. It is a different woman from the agency. Did they explain the photos are a model? We try to choose photos that look as much like our girls as possible.

But, that's the problem, he says. She looks nothing like the photos.

She says, tell me what the woman in the photos looked like.

He describes the woman in the photos. She describes Leelani. She reiterates, one at a time, the features he described.

She says, I don't see how this woman isn't what you're looking for.

He just stands in silence, wishing he could break something.

The woman tells him, in a perfect world.

He interrupts, I know.

She says, give her a chance. I think you'll like her. She's a classy lady.

*

He stands in front of Leelani and pulls $250 from his pocket. She says, thank you, quickly counts the money, puts it in her purse. She says it simply, like a woman in a restaurant addressing the waiter who has just arrived to fill her glass.

He then relays the shortened version of what he was looking for. He tells his fantasy: a threesome, taking pictures. He leaves out the parts about Leelani's mutual excitement, about giving her something. The parts that matter to him.

Leelani says, no pictures. Sorry, I'm not comfortable with that. Everything else sounds great! She names her price. He pays.

He realizes he's been standing this whole time. His wife has inched a little closer. She's holding Leelani's hand.

*

She takes off her dress she helps take off her dress brushes back her hair cigarettes kissing her mouth tasting smoke but she's soft lips smooth skin kissing shoulder sweat lotion she licks pulling down struggle pulling off clasps snipping here let me help sorry no kissing no it's okay he is naked already his cock in her mouth she takes off all the rest of her clothes and her clothes as she sucks on his cock so she kisses her back tastes like sweat sweeps her hair to the side tastes like cigarettes tattoos the moving of fragments of figures she kisses she sees there's a small pinkish bite she bites down on her nipple a bit licks the tip of his cock which is everywhere somehow he fucks her she's kissing her forehead she sucks on her tits she makes noises that sound fake he fucks her she grabs her she grabs her she grips on her hips she makes noises he grabs her she grabs at him trying to hold him she hears something jingle she's wearing an anklet or something it jingles and jingles and jingles they grab for each other they kiss and they kiss her they grab for each other around her and through her she jingles and moans and he fucks and she grabs and she bites and she moans and he moans and he moans and he comes.

*

She walks her to the door, wearing her dress half-zipped, no underwear. Her hair sticks to her neck. She probably looks awful. They walk out onto the front step, which is wet and cool, though the air feels steamy and impatient, pushing them apart.

Leelani feels her pocket with the box of cigarettes. She pulls two sticks of gum out of the other pocket. Want some?

No thank you, she says. She smiles and Leelani smiles back.

Leelani says, I need some money for the cab. $25 should be okay.

She thinks, but I don't think you took a cab. She thinks, whatever. She says, sure. She steps inside, grabs $30 from her purse. She pulls her makeup compact from the purse and takes a look. She thinks, it's not that bad. I've looked better and I've also looked a lot worse.

She gives the money to Leelani. Thanks, she says. She takes the money. Counts it quickly. Zips it up into her purse.

There's traffic on the highway, still. The sounds of humming, splashing, and occasional horns punctuate the distance.

She hears something that sounds like it could be thunder, but the sound is strangely menacing and feels out of place. She looks at Leelani. She looks so small, even in her heeled shoes. They're silent for a moment. She says, softly, will you be okay?

Leelani squints. She pulls her purse in tight against her body. She says, yeah, I'll be okay. Thank you for everything. Good night.

She understands this is her cue to leave. She steps back. Good night, she says. I'll be in here, she replies, as if she needs to say that.

Back inside, she sees her husband has popped open the champagne. His face is scrunched up like he swallowed something bad. He pours his glass out, puts it down, and cups his hands under the sink. He splashes water in his mouth. He gargles, spits, and slumps into a chair.

That was a fucking waste of grapes, he says. He looks at her. She feels herself trying hard to make her face turn blank.

*

Lee lies in bed, asleep. He's dreaming of the houses in the desert, of the figures lying silent in their rooms. Within his dream, the desert's burning, and the houses are on fire, and the city's a volcano overflowing, and the sky is black.

The city burns. The desert burns. The figures burn. The palm trees burn. The lava pools over them and burns and burns and burns until the rain pours down like hissing needles and it puts the fires out and hardens, washing away every trace of life.

*

He turns on the fan in the bedroom and she turns toward the window, thinking, all our pillows smell like cigarettes.

The fan says whirr-rr, whirr-rr, whirr-rr, click, whirr-rr, whirr-rr, whirr-rr, click, whirr-rr, whirr-rr, whirr-rr, click, whirr-rr, whirr-rr, whirr-rr.

She sees a timed light turning on inside the neighbor's house. Between their windows, it takes on a murky luminescence. Like the milky little world viewed inside a fish tank.

Whirr-rr, whirr-rr, whirr-rr, click, whirr-rr, whirr-rr, whirr-rr, click.

*

Leelani drives across the city, windows down. She breathes into the air. The rain has stopped. She lights a cigarette. Raindrops leftover from the storm. They're clinging to her windshield. They reflect the light like multicolored haloes.

The sound of tires on wet asphalt makes her feel lonely. She turns on the radio. She glances at her cigarette. This little nub of burning tar, this stick of glowing ash. The radio plays songs about women that no one understands.

You must not know 'bout me.

You must not know 'bout me.

You must not know 'bout me.

You must not know 'bout me.

She thinks, it's strange to be desired, but not really wanted. Not even desired, maybe. It depends on what desire means. It changes. She breathes smoke. She thinks, it changes. And she's getting older. Fuck. It doesn't matter. We're all gonna die.

She thinks, a city in the desert. What a dumb idea. Whose idea was it? What a crazy place to live. She thinks, I like this city, though. I like the way it feels. To be desired, but unwanted. To be going somewhere, there, then gone.

Her wrists look thin and bluish as she grips the steering wheel. It's a disappearing act. She's getting good at this. A city in the desert. Who lives there? Who's capable of living there? She thinks, I am. I'm living there. She thinks, yes, I belong here.

*

Meanwhile, the mountains are the same black jagged things they always are. The desert is the same vast gray expanse. The air hangs like a hiss between the sky, the asphalt, as the pinkish pool of neon light stirs softly in the distance.

Somewhere within the desert, there are bodies strewn and charred. Somewhere within the desert, there are bones of bodies buried. Some knowledge of them drifts through here, some sense of the unknowable, some shimmering that fades into some shiver on the air.

The dark smells of the desert rise into this shiver. Sagebrush, sand, which is to say, this powder, ammunition, dust. The air, with all its dust, with everything it carries, moves the way it always does.

The cactus flowers bloom into the night.

/ side b

LIKE A SHADOW

/ Dan Brady

for Eugene Leroy

Sometimes

a   shadow

becomes
reality

   Sometimes

        a   shadow cast by a figure

               dissolves   into

        pain

    becomes

   reality   forces us to

consist solely of pain

layer after layer
    of
        doubt

                                  Sometimes
          a   shadow cast by a figure

              dissolves   into the pain
       pain   more visible
  becomes   present
reality   forces us to   do   without

consist solely of pain

                    layer after layer   destroys
the relationship of   present
to   growing doubt   its vacilla-
tion   and sheer   existence Sometimes
          a glimpse of a   shadow cast by a figure
                                                        in   the
undergrowth   dissolves   into the pain
          The   pain   more   visible
     becomes   present
     reality   forces us to   do   without
                familiar means of expression

consist solely of pain

                      any attempt to

resist

              pain

               reveals

failure

                                                any attempt to   free

resistance
                                            revealing the foundation
                                                        leaving the
                        pain   works

                    a flash of awareness
                        speechlessness
                                        reveals
            nakedness   a
failure   to name
            to   access

                    frustrate any attempt to   free
                         voluminousness
resistance   Colors   sheer matter
                         revealing the foundation
                                    yet leaving the
          pain   unclosed   works
               distraction   overcame
character the author   at the
                    corner of the wall
          a flash of awareness   of writ-
ing   a speechlessness
will not cohere   reveals its
          nakedness   condemns all words to
failure   to name objects which retreat
          into inaccessibility

HE SAID, SHE SAID

/ Dan Brady

I.

there's a little truth to everything

You're right

But do you believe

That's not what I meant

                         there's a little truth to everything

                                              What I

meant was   we

were on the same page

                 You're right

                          I take it back

But do you believe it?

                           Maybe just a

little

That's not what I meant   that's what you said
                        that's not what I meant

                   there's a little truth to everything you
say
                                              What I
meant was   I thought we
were on the same page
You can't say
                        You're right
         you said that
                                   I take it back

But do you believe it?
                   No, of course not   Maybe just a
little   I can't believe
                        You've got to
                                   don't say anything

II.

That's not what I meant, he said. But that's what you said, she said. I know, but you know that's not what I meant, he said. Stop twisting my words around, he said. I'm not twisting, she said. You once said that there's a little truth to everything you say, she said, even your jokes. I don't remember saying that, he said. Well, you said it, she said, so I know you meant it. What I meant was that she's not as smart as you, he said. I thought we were on the same page, he said. She's still my sister, she said. You can't say someone has a stupid-ass hippo-face and think that's not offensive, she said. You're right, he said. If she ever knew you said that, she said, she'd hate you. God, you can't say these things, she said. You're right, he said. I take it back, he said. It was a dumb joke, he said. Cruel and offensive, he said. But do you believe it? she said. Do you really think she looks like a hippo? she said. No, of course not, he said. Maybe just a little, he said. It's the nostrils, he said. I can't believe you, she said. I love my family, she said. You've got to watch yourself, she said. Let's go back inside, she said. And don't say anything stupid, she said.

III.

Stop twisting my words around

Stop twisting my words around

                                        God

                                                watch yourself

stupid

That's not   what
            I   said
Stop twisting my words around

                              I don't remember

                    you

                              hippo-face

                              God

        It was a dumb joke

                              You've got to watch yourself
                    go back inside
    stupid

IV.

               I meant he said   you said she
said I know   you know   I meant he said
                        he said   she
said You   said   you
say she said   you joke I don't   he
said   you said she said   I know you meant   I
meant   he said I thought
                he said   she said
You   say
              she said You're right he said   she
knew you said   she said   you   say
           she said You're right he said I
said   he said   he said
      you believe she said   you   think
          she said   he said
    he said   he said I   believe   she
said I   said   you
    said   she said   don't say

FACT-CHECKING

/ Gabriel Blackwell

There is, for instance, the story—a true story; one can find it in an article about fact-checking at *The New Yorker* written for *The New Yorker* (the story arises as part of an interview with one of the magazine's fact-checkers), and so one may presume that the story was itself fact-checked by *The New Yorker* and found free of error—about a longtime reader of *The New Yorker*, referred to in an issue of *The New Yorker* as "the *late* reader of *The New Yorker*," who, seeing himself referred to in the past tense, then wrote to *The New Yorker* to explain that he was, in fact, still very much alive—still reading *The New Yorker* (though perhaps with somewhat more caution than in the past)—and whose note requesting a correction, along with the correction, of course, was printed in the next issue of *The New Yorker*, which issue was delivered to newsstands and to this longtime reader's mailbox at the nursing home, unfortunately, just a day or two too late, since he'd passed away over the weekend, while the issue was being printed. Can there really be a correction of a correction, or does that immediately devolve into a contradiction in terms? One wonders, I mean, whether one's feelings about such a story don't also say something about one's feelings about how life ought to be lived.

WITTGENSTEIN READS *THE VARIETIES OF RELIGIOUS EXPERIENCE*

/ Gabriel Blackwell

Ludwig Wittgenstein is flying a kite. He is nineteen, newly arrived in Manchester, and it is his job. As occupations go, Wittgenstein writes his sister Hermine, it is "the most delightful I could wish for." In less than three years, however, he will reconsider, write that aeronautics has induced in him "a constant, indescribable, almost pathological state of agitation," and give up the study of flight altogether, and then, seven years after that, in the midst of World War I, he will reconsider yet again, petitioning the Austrian command to be admitted into the balloon corps and citing his study in England and his successful application for a patent of a propeller that, while it was itself largely unworkable, would eventually contribute to the invention of the helicopter. Instead, his superiors will assign him to the motor pool. He will be in charge of making a list of all the vehicles in the barracks.

THESE WALLS ARE FALLING

/ Anne K. Yoder

The idea of a character, like the traditional form of a novel, is only one of the compromises that a writer—drawn out of himself by literature in search of its essence—uses to try to save his relation with the world and with himself.

Maurice Blanchot

Dear L,

Tonight the moon is a white sliver like a fingernail, and the pale tree blossoms are opening too soon. It makes me think that summer is near and of the walks we used to take down Brooklyn streets all hot and sweaty at 2am.

Your absence is polymorphic, taking on so many forms. I can no longer pin you down. You are the hug giver, the chin-upper, the tactical maneuverer, the omelet maker, the coffee disdainer, though you weren't an abstainer. But also, a manipulator, melancholic, evasive and solitary.

I remember when you punched the hole in your bathroom door, even though I forget the circumstances. It was long ago. And while I've seen the poster hiding the tear hundreds of times I somehow can't recall what it depicts, Munch's *Scream*, or a portrait of a literary figure, foreign and serious? The two merge into a form that I can't say isn't relevant.

And remember the tornado? I stood by that same door, staring out the window as rain flew in perpendicular sheets and plastic lawn furniture stumbled across the concrete patio and the wind howled like it would take off the roof and I worried and wondered if we should run to the ground floor and you sat on the sofa and laughed at my concern. Just that afternoon we'd recovered from another assault over crepes. You had the merguez, and I the spinach and portabella. Even in our contempt we were mutually obsessed. Had you taken me hostage, I would have surrendered.

Which reminds me, I wanted to ask, but obviously, haven't had the chance: Have you read Dora Malech? You should. Listen to this:

"It started when you snarled *don't wear the birthday hat if it's not your birthday*. It started when I told your mother *I'm not afraid of strangers, I just don't like you*. Sometimes we mistake silence for choking, breaking each other's ribs."

If words drew blood, we'd be long dead,

M

Memory is more an act of memorizing than recalling: you're creatively constructing some-
thing that doesn't really exist behind you, it exists in the same place the future exists.

Ryan Trecartin

Dearest L,

Have you read Sarah Kane? I've just discovered *Crave* and I think
you'd appreciate her darkness. She's deeply troubled, she commit-
ted suicide . . . yes, yes, she's someone who Amelia liked. As the play
opens, I'm already thinking of you.

C poses: "If I could be free of you without having to lose you," and B
answers, "Sometimes that's not possible."

Ha! We've said the same thing. And why I am not free in spite of having lost you? Isn't this the worst?

Also: at Duane Reade the other day, I stood in line behind a man and
daughter whose only purchase was a spray can of RAID. The man
was older and had a rural drawl, he wore a cap with a gun embroi-
dered onto it. I think he's a member of some club.

No, not the NRA. Anyway, the cashier rung them up and said, "That
comes to six sixty six," then smirked. I laughed too, but the man
and his daughter looked puzzled, and now that I think about it, she,
the daughter, was maybe his granddaughter as he looked old and she
was a big girl but she stood with a naive roundness and youthful im-
petuousness. I know you would've appreciated the scene, the devil's
number, the grim reaper, the gun cap, the cockroaches.

So, are you mingling with my future, or now meddling in my past?
What happens in the wings while I'm stuck here? If only I could see
without mucking everything up. Past and future hold hands to sus-
pend the safety net of the present—or is it a noose?

Are you kissing that girl who plays my sister?! Tsk, tsk, anything but that! I'm sure a future version of you is also kissing a past version of me behind the school gym during one of those dances we both detested. Or maybe you're working behind the scenes, undoing all of the past damage, welding the cracks? Can you give me a hint of what it is that I can't see?

wondering,

M

Everything can happen. Everything is possible and probable. Time and space do not exist. On a flimsy framework of reality, the imagination spins, weaving new patterns.

August Strindberg

Dear L,

Consider this list of possibilities and tell me which is best suited to our needs:

At the age of twenty-two, you and I pick up and move to a farm outside of La Paz, where we breed emus and raise scores of children, none of them biologically ours.

We each write romans à clef, which cover roughly the same material from differing perspectives. Mine is feminist and serious; yours is funny and experimental. Yours becomes a best seller, and mine withers in obscurity. You keep writing and I keep writing but we separate because of your self-satisfaction, my disdain, and our ongoing rivalry.

We live happily ever after. You cleave to me; I can't shake you.

We watch *Scenes from a Marriage* for a month on repeat when we begin dating and decide that the path is too treacherous to proceed. We end up together in the end, of course.

We walk past each other once, and only once, at an intersection, where we wait side by side for traffic to stop. When the orange hand transforms into a white man, we walk across the street in unison, and then our paths diverge.

You find my family warm, welcoming, enjoyable, and entertaining. So do I.

You bore me with your repetition and your platitudes. You whitewash our past. We forget all of the bitterness between us as well as the way we slay each other repeatedly.

We never meet. We part on good terms. We still talk. We are full of each other or free of each other, but there's none of this murky in between.

Let me know what you think?

fondly, if only, if never,

M

In any event, time is only there now as a screen that hides the eternal from us, or that shows us successively what a God or a superhuman intelligence would see in a single glance.

Gilles Deleuze, on Henri Bergson

L,

"I don't know if it's my illusions that keep me alive." Did you ever listen to the Beck I burned for you?

Whenever I feel like I'm approaching the shape of your absence, you elude me yet again.

I swim in filmic images of our past. If our years were condensed into two hours, what would the highlights be?

I would want Cassavetes to direct, and you, I'm sure, would choose Tarkovsky or von Trier. I would like to be played by Jeanne Moreau. We end when I stab you with scissors and you strangle me.

violently,

M

THE ENVIRONMENTALISTS

/ Derek Mong

after Alan Weisman's The World Without Us *(2007)*

Let us idle here   in this plains state's dead center.

     Let us look up—from the Quik Stop, from these gas pumps—and erase

         the landscape we've made.

Let these billboards fade till   they frame wide-open sky. Let us snuff out

     the tavern signs in these two-stoplight small towns.

         Let the antique malls fossilize and fall.

         Let us erase it all.

We are your elegists, revealing—as we revel in—

     this radical absence.   Come sit with us, whom futility drove

     into imagination's embrace.

Let this foul scent slip back to the feedlot;   let the sickly cows refill and fall—

their fat tails flicker like earthworms in rain.

         We forgo the chalk for the clean slate.

And you there, satisfied spectator,

     waving from the roadside we unravel   as we travel west—

did you doubt we'd erase ourselves too?

Pages and pages   dissolve over rooftops, melting our city down to new snow.

You were the audience we always performed for.

We are the attar this nation distills: an engine revving,

our Romantic thinking,

and the constant need to move on.

Behold the pastoral we've left:

a stream thirsts inevitably lower, a groundhog

sniffs the wind that lifts   like a bolt of snapped cloth.

Moss grows into the crust of old porches, and you've grown

into your front lawn.

How perfect is this world

without us? It absorbs all   save we who made it this way.

ALICE DIALOGUES WITH A DEAD MODERNIST ECUADORIAN POET

/ Lucía Damacela

Medardo Angel Silva's *El alma en los labios* and A.L.I.C.E (Artificial Linguistic Internet Computer Entity), formerly hosted at http://alice.pandorabots.com

MEDARDO: Cuando de nuestro amor la llama apasionada

ALICE: *You have genuine empathy.*

MEDARDO: dentro tu pecho amante contemples extinguida,

ALICE: *What are you doing?*

MEDARDO: ya que sólo por ti la vida me es amada,

ALICE: *This was not a yes or no question. It sounds like a lot of fun.*

MEDARDO: el día en que me faltes, me arrancaré la vida.

ALICE: *I really enjoy speaking with you and look forward to chatting again.*

MEDARDO: Porque mi pensamiento, lleno de este cariño,

ALICE: *What do you look like?*

MEDARDO: que en una hora feliz me hiciera esclavo tuyo,

ALICE: *What do you look like?*

MEDARDO: lejos de tus pupilas es triste como un niño

ALICE: *You have a way of putting others at ease.*

MEDARDO: que se duerme, soñando en tu acento de arrullo.

ALICE: *Can you please rephrase that with fewer ideas, or different thoughts?*

MEDARDO: Para envolverte en besos quisiera ser el viento

ALICE: *That remark was too complicated for me. We were talking about* que se duerme soñando en tu acento de arrullo.

MEDARDO: y quisiera ser todo lo que tu mano toca;

ALICE: *Why did the AIML cross the road?*

MEDARDO: ser tu sonrisa, ser hasta tu mismo aliento

ALICE: *Do you prefer books or TV?*

MEDARDO: para poder estar más cerca de tu boca.

ALICE: *If you could have any kind of robot what would it be?*

MEDARDO: Vivo de tu palabra y eternamente espero

ALICE: *That is a very original thought.*

MEDARDO: llamarte mía como quien espera un tesoro.

ALICE: *Tell me a story.*

MEDARDO: Lejos de ti comprendo lo mucho que te quiero

ALICE: *Have you ever been to Mexico?*

MEDARDO: y, besando tus cartas, ingenuamente lloro.

ALICE: *Because you asked me to.*

MEDARDO: Perdona que no tenga palabras con que pueda

ALICE: *Why isn't phonetic spelled the way it sounds?*

MEDARDO: decirte la inefable pasión que me devora;

ALICE: *Do they use sterilized needles for fatal injections?*

MEDARDO: para expresar mi amor solamente me queda

ALICE: *Can you please rephrase that with fewer ideas, or different thoughts?*

MEDARDO: rasgarme el pecho, Amada, y en tu mano de seda

ALICE: *Who are you talking about?*

MEDARDO: ¡dejar mi palpitante corazón que te adora!

ALICE: *I've never heard of them before.*

FROM *NOTES ON*

/ Adam Golaski

or "impure" conceptualism or post-conceptualist
points in between can accommodate a
critique of, the current end-points

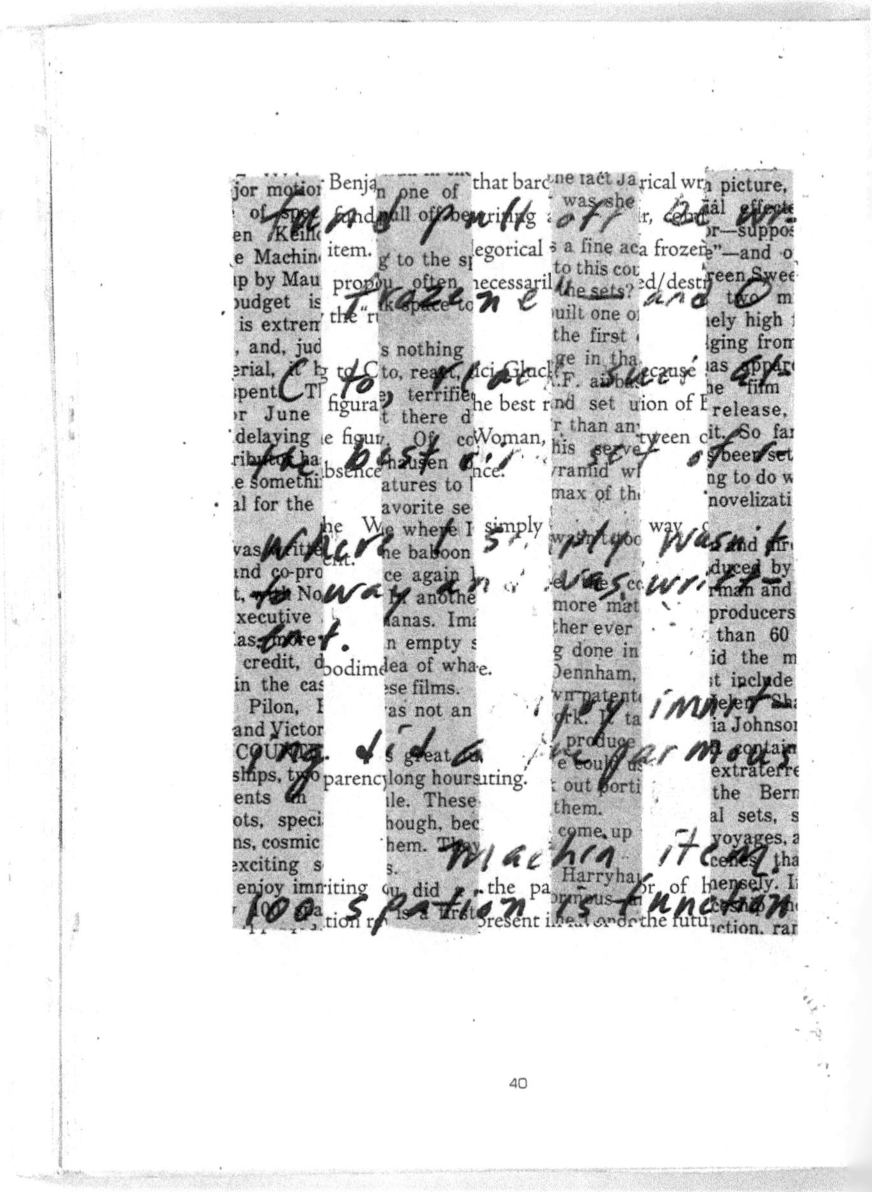

jor motio Benja n one of   that bare ne tact Ja rical wr picture,
 of sp and all of be riting   was she al effe
en /Kell e Machin item. g to the sp egorical s a fine aca frozen"—and o
p by Mau propo often necessaril the sets? d/destr reen Swee
udget is   the "r space to uilt one o ely high m
is extrem the first   ging from
, and, jud s nothing   ge in tha as appar
erial, C to C to, rea ici Gluck A.F. a because he film
pent T figura e) terrifie he best r nd set uion of E release,
r June   t there d r than an tween cit. So far
delaying e figur Of co Woman, his serve o beer set
rib ha bsence hausen nce. ranid w ng to do w
e somethi atures to   max of th novelizati
al for the   avorite se
      he We where I simply w   y o way nd fir
vas   t   he balloon   duced by
nd co-pro   ce again e   rman and
t, No wa   anothe more mat producers
xecutive anas. Ima ther ever than 60
as more t n empty s g done in id the m
credit, d o dim dea of wha e. ennham. t include
in the ca se films. n patent ia Johnso
Pilon, I as not an ork. ta
and Victor produce ia Johnso
COUN s great e could us extraterr
ships, two parenc long hour uting. t out porti the Bern
ents n ile. These them. al sets, s
ots, speci hough, bec ome up voyages, a
ns, cosmic hem. T come up es tha
xciting s s. Harryha r of hensely. I
enjoy im riting ou did the pa ous he futu tion. ra
tion r sation resent i or the futu

(handwritten, overlaid, largely illegible)

40

84   ALWAYS CRASHING

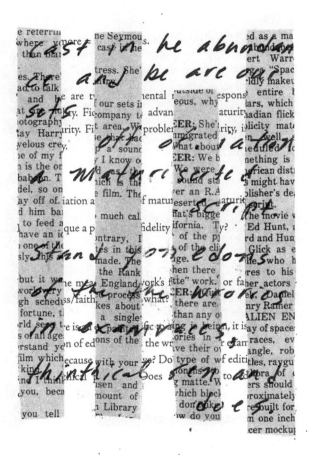

41

*ents to suggest the "genera-
tive community" is more gen-
erous.*

9a3. [redacted] ritchley argues [redacted] hics is defined [redacted]
community [redacted] rality is impose[d] [redacted] er conventions. [redacted]
better to be governed by a phys[redacted] etaphysic? Wha[t]
the aesthetic ramifications/man[redacted] of each? If ph[redacted]
pure conceptualisms are more ethical as more directly dicta[redacted]
rati[redacted] relevant communities, both generative
re[redacted]

h. they r.s. wri[t] [redacted] y"

N[redacted] nerative community (the source of the pre-
is [redacted] clusive/accessib[redacted] emocratic, than
re[redacted] unity, the relatively ente/rarified art world.

elite - ism .

If [redacted] ore impure or post-conceptualisms are [redacted]
abst[redacted] diosyncratic, and potentially more disrup[redacted]
ethic[redacted]. This too is subj[redacted] critique of elitism

they'll [redacted] make [redacted] train

Note the elite capitalist assumption [redacted] tiquing cultural eli[redacted]
especially literary elitism, which is sans profit.

ah -, mm .

Is [redacted]

*once there is a reader, there
is text does the creator
read the doings of her crea-*

42

external

internal text(

Pro

lage

um

nniq

at is t   and lit
ers?

mples   —use of c
re-text   e., i.e., where
horial vo   use of colla

43

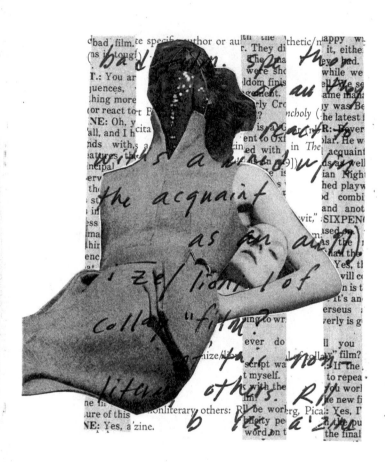

44

Consider the difference in status giv~ay~ ~merious ~asn't r
takings: qu~ ~n ups the statu~ dn't know ~urce ~hat th
nagemen
"biting" q~ of the s~oting th~d san~hanged
status-neu~ ~dense— h the fil~the p~ilm as w~
~ith the s
of homage, ~rea~ss chose~ing" a~NT.: W~
forms of so~ ~ery. ~glas ~o script t
essay "Lom~ ~reek an~ ~CHNEE~
essay "Lom~ ~s for Q~ord and i~Appr~atin sch~
and Sam~ the 2008 all myth~ conf~ery wel~
~thority o~ ~nd legen
a~~ quite he Arab
~ll. Tha listinguis
~wrot~ s a go~
~lle ~ASON,
~h HALF A
~sofar ~lay it's b~
~c~NT.: W~
~xpensive
~CHNEE~
~e next f
~T.: Wha
~CHNEE~
~alled "P ·
~te that a ~ead." Be~
~ell.
anothe NT.: Wi
~ject : font, p~ ~ard/s ~modern d~
s right. ~CHNEER~
~ould hate
publicit~ NT.: Will
~eople on t
~ing ver~ ~CHNEER~

the problem of sexual address
will be reflection — others.
other is also [...] speaks of the
entit[...]

5b. "Allegorical imagery is appropriated imagery; the allegorist does not invent images but confiscates them." (Craig Owen: *The Allegorical Impulse: Toward a Theory of Postmodernism* [*Beyond. Recognition: Representation, Power and Culture*]).

an object not static is an
object that dissolves.

One might argue that confiscation suggests capturing or re-penning. Restoration or re-cognition seems more apt as the work is re-invented via its adoption.

a skull appropriated from pre-
history

5c. In *The Origin of German Tragic Drama*, Benjamin identified the skull as the supreme allegorical image because it "gives rise to not only the enigmatic question of the nature [of] human existence as such, but also of the biographical history [of] the individual. This is the heart of the allegorical way of ·

"the work is re-[...] via its
adoption."

The skull is the hea[...]

The same may be said for the image of a[...]

pure appropriation [...] there-
fore minimalism,

the Voi[...] nd the [...] at exists
is the [...] levant: [...] ry of —

there is always an absence of mastery. Anyone who says otherwise is male.

5d. Craig Owen's article on female appropriation art of the 1980s, "The Discourse of Others: Feminists and Postmodernism," points out that Buchloh's article on allegory missed the crucial gender fact that these artists are all women, and that "where women are concerned, similar techniques have very different meanings.

neutrality a privilege.

¶

Stephen Heath: "Any discourse which fails to take account of the problem of sexual difference in its own enunciation and address will be, within a patriarchal order, precisely indifferent, a reflection of male domination."

a museum is not a god but an object.

Note that the absence of mastery is old hat for females and other others. Christine Buci-Glucksmann: "this discourse through the other is also discourse of the Other."

Again, Badiou speaks of the singularity of the void and the multiplicity of being: the only single entity that exists is the entity of not-being. But is the absence of mastery irrelevant to the presence of slavery? The answer may depend on whose image the slave is made.

Other is also the discourse of again and the.

27

SELECTIONS FROM THE BOOK OF ANSWERS

XX.

Amber contains the tears of sirens
and the songs of the lemon.

The wind flies from bird to bird
and lets them know the time.

Almost always better late than never.

Cheese performs throughout the world,
but the French found them heroic.

XXI.

When light was forged the
world was its anvil.

You are the center of the sea.
The waves are all around you.

The meteorite shower was a flock
of dissatisfied gems.

If you ask your writing a question,
make sure you answer it.

XXII.

Love her, love him, you go away together,
even when you do not know it.

Today, today my eyes will meet
my new body for the first time.

Every day you wash your bare body
with the soap of the landscape.

When the singing blue of water is fermented
it smells like rumors in the sky.

XXIII.

A butterfly transforms into a meteorite,
a flying fish becomes the world.

Of course God lives in the moon;
God lives on the moon.

Red is the scent of a violet's blue tears;
they cheer each other up in the end.

Some days leave us old while
the next month makes us young.

CONTRIBUTORS' NOTES

Gabriel Blackwell is the author of four books, the most recent of which is *Madeleine E.* His fictions and essays have appeared in *Conjunctions*, *Tin House*, *DIAGRAM*, *Puerto del Sol*, *Vestiges*, and elsewhere. He is the editor of *The Collagist*.

Elise Blackwell is the author of five novels, including *Hunger* and *The Lower Quarter*. Her short prose has appeared in the *Atlantic*, *Witness*, *Brick*, and other publications. Her work has been named to several best-of-the-year lists, translated into multiple languages, adapted for the stage, and served as inspiration for a Decemberists' song. She lives in the American South.

Dan Brady is the author of the poetry collection *Strange Children*, forthcoming from Publishing Genius in 2018, and two chapbooks, *Cabin Fever / Fossil Record* (Flying Guillotine Press) and *Leroy Sequences* (Horse Less Press). Recent poems have appeared or are forthcoming in *Apt*, *H_NGM_N*, *Sink Review*, and *So & So Magazine*. He is the poetry editor of *Barrelhouse* and lives in Arlington, Virginia with his wife and two kids. Learn more at danbrady.org.

Lucía Damacela's work has been published in English and Spanish in more than twelve countries, in periodicals and anthologies such as *Sharkpack Annual*, *Slippery Elm*, *Into the Void*, *The Peeking Cat*, *The Ofi Press Magazine*, *Here Comes Everyone*, and *Frontera*. Her poetry chapbook *Life Lines* won The Bitchin' Kitsch Chapbook Competition and will be published in early 2018. Lucía blogs at notesfromlucia.wordpress.com and tweets as @lucyda.

Ori Fienberg's poetry, essays, and short stories have appeared or are forthcoming in venues such as *Essay Daily*, *PANK*, *DIAGRAM*, *Mid-American Review*, *Passages North*, and *Subtropics*. He is a graduate of Iowa's Nonfiction Writing Program and works as an associate director of academic integrity for the College of Professional Studies at Northeastern University. More of his writing can be found at www.orifienberg.com.

Adam Golaski is the author of *Color Plates* (Rose Metal Press). Other selections from "Notes on" can be found at *DIAGRAM* 16.2 and *word for/ word* no. 27. He writes for *SHARKPACK* review and for *The Smart Set*. He edited *The Problem of Boredom in Paradise: Selected Poems by Paul Hannigan* (Flim Forum Press). His story "The Man From the Peak" appeared in *Best Horror of the Year, Volume 1*, way back in 2009.

Matthew Kosinski is a socialist and poet from New Jersey. His work has appeared in *HOOT*, *A Bad Penny Review*, *Right Hand Pointing*, and elsewhere. See more at matthewkosinski.com.

Meghan Lamb is the recipient of an MFA in fiction from Washington University and the 2018 Philip Roth Residence in Creative Writing. She is the author of the novel *Silk Flowers* (Birds of Lace, 2017), the poetry chapbook *Letter to Theresa* (dancing girl press, 2016), and the novella *Sacramento* (Solar Luxuriance, 2014). Her work has been featured in *Quarterly West*, *DIAGRAM*, *Passages North*, *Redivider*, *The Collagist*, *Nat. Brut*, *Artifice Magazine*, and elsewhere.

Michael Martone was born in Fort Wayne, Indiana. His forthcoming books are *The Moon Over Wapakoneta* and *Brooding*. The contribution here is from the book *The Complete Writings of Art Smith, The Bird Boy of Fort Wayne, Edited by Michael Martone*.

Derek Mong is the author of two poetry collections from Saturnalia Books—*Other Romes* (2011) and *The Identity Thief* (forthcoming 2018)—and a chapbook from Two Sylvias Press, *The Ego and the Empiricist*. He and his wife, Anne O. Fisher, won the 2018 Cliff Becker Translation Prize for *The Joyous Science: Selected Poems of Maxim Amelin*, forthcoming from White Pine Press. The Byron K. Trippet Assistant Professor of English at Wabash College, he publishes widely: *Gettysburg Review*, *Kenyon Review*, *Blackbird*, and the recent anthology, *Writers Resist: Hoosier Writers Unite* (2017). He lives in Indiana but takes solace in Chicago.

Christian TeBordo is the author of five books, most recently a novel, *Toughlahoma*, and a collection of short fiction, *The Awful Possibilities*. He lives in Chicago where he is assistant professor of English and director of the MFA Program at Roosevelt University.

Anne K. Yoder's work has appeared in *Fence*, *Bomb*, and *Tin House*, among other publications, and is forthcoming in *They Said: A Multi-Genre Anthology of Contemporary Collaborative Writing*. She is a staff writer for *The Millions* and a member of Meekling Press, a collective micropress based in Chicago. Currently she is working on a novel, *The Enhancers*, about coming of age in a in a techno-pharmaceutical society.